The Death Of Humanity
A Science Fiction Thriller
By Jaysen True Blood

How It Began

I t was so easy for them to supplant us as the dominant species of Earth. And they seemed so perfect. So godlike.

We were so busy warring over politics. Supremacy of color. Religion. Greed. Hate. Personal preferences.

They only had to read our thoughts and use them against us. They became the return of Christ to the most religious claiming to be Christian. Or the promised Messiah for those practicing Judaism. Or the returning Mohammed. Or Shiva the Destroyer. Or whichever god the people were hoping for in the region they landed.

Hell. They only had to claim to be the solution to the political corruption we suffered at the hands of our human masters. Or the solution to the world's greed.

They could have claimed *anything* and humanity would have fallen in line. After all, the most desperate were the most ignorant. The most hateful were the most ignorant.

Our political systems had failed. The politicians had sold out to corporate religion and corporate slaveholders. Wages were abysmal, so low that a wage earner could not truly live without worry of starvation or eviction. Education was incomplete and obsolete, teaching the old but never remaining relevant.

The only constant in Human life was greed and hate. Those who had greedily hogged assets needed by all and hated those who worked for them. The average man greedily worked his life away and hated those he was told were taking jobs, despite the fact that corporations had been sending jobs overseas for decades. And the poorer a man was, the more he hated those who weren't like him because his religion and his political gods told him to hate them.

Amid this, they came. Perfect in every way, from human perception. They came neither feasting nor drinking. Their words, true and pure to the listener but meant to mislead. Meant to deceive.

And they *did* claim to be the promised return of the gods. The answer to all of the planet's ills. And we *did* fall right in line. At first.

Well, most of us did. I did not. Nor did those who were my close associates.

Why I would be thrust into the role of hero was beyond me. I was not the hero type. In fact, I was overweight, over the age, and in ill health. I was, for all intents and purposes, ill suited for the calling.

And my friends and associates were a ragtag group of computer geeks, small business owners, and young entrepreneurs who had not yet fallen to the wiles of greed. Most were, after all, in the arts. Authors. Sculptors. Musicians. Painters. Actors.

But all ran their own businesses. Some were struggling, in the current economy, to rise from the red but all were still in business. And none had been tainted by greed.

And all saw through the illusion. We saw through the disguise the aliens used. They were not human. They were not benevolent.

Most of all, they were not the saviors they claimed to be. They wanted to subjugate. Enslave.

They wanted to use man as their new food source. All but those they felt could be used as their 'representatives' who would placate and lull the masses into a numbness that would hide the horrors that awaited. Of course, these 'representatives' would also serve as executioners of all who could see through the aliens' lies and illusions.

I SUPPOSE I OUGHT TO begin at the beginning. How it happened. Where they came from. Why they came.

It was election year. America was more divided than it had ever been. Insecure men ran the streets with automatic rifles on their backs, homegrown terrorist organizations had validation they had never earned through a president who did not win the election four years before, and protests were happening everywhere. Fringe religious groups had backed the worst possible candidate, falling from grace in the public eye....not that they had been in good graces with the public, they had not.

These religious groups wanted to bring on a twisted and demented version of whet they believed the 'kingdom of God' would be, where everyone was forced to believe in a lie. *Their lie.*

The political parties were so corrupt that they no longer did the will of the people. And yet, the people voted for them because they believed the political lies and half-truths. but mostly lies...just like the religions of the world. All lies.

Science had been probing space for another earth-like planet, one that could possibly sustain human life, and had found a multitude. But one had caught their eye and they probed it with sound beams. And they had received an answer.

We are listening. We are watching. We are waiting.

That had been the answer. Short. Eerie. To the point.

But the team passed it off as a practical joke. They believed it to be a hack. And yet, they could not explain why the source had been located on the planet they had sent the message to.

A few days later, the message was followed by another.

We are ready. We are coming. We will be arriving.

We are here.

FIVE BILLION LIGHT years from Earth lay a planet under siege. The aliens had come, they said, in peace. To bring peace and unity to the planet. They had brought war and more death instead.

The inhabitants of the planet realized, a bit too late, that the aliens intended to use them for food and as slave labor.

These aliens had no homeworld. No point of origin that could be pointed to on any map of the known universe.

They had destroyed their own planet through war and overuse. Leaving, they became predatory scavengers. What they couldn't scavenge, they got through preying on other races.

Once their planet had been destroyed by a supernova, they were forced into interstellar migration. Planet to planet. Galaxy to galaxy. Until they reached the planet Earth's scientists had sent a transmission to.

There, they had waged a war for over a billion years against a resistance greater than any they had ever experienced. Then opportunity, in the form of a probe message from Earth, knocked. After all, they had always followed what they saw as distress signals from young planets where the occupants sought out intelligent life.

Distress, in the form of a probe. Distress that was not always distress. Distress in the form of curiosity. Deadly curiosity.

It Came Out Of The Sky

It was dawn when the team from SETI and those from NASA witnessed the ship's entry into the atmosphere and began settling upon the coordinates that had been sent to them by the visitors. The president, politicians from both parties, every religious leader in the country, and those who believed the visitors to be God returning to claim his 'kingdom were also present. Millions more watched in awed horror as humanity's fate came silently from the sky.

The scene was very much the same elsewhere in the world. Europe. Asia. Africa. The Middle East. Australia and the south Pacific.

"Yam," the lead visitor stated without moving his humanoid lips, "That I am."

"Yah," Another began, "that I am. Weh be my title."

"Jesu," another moved to the front of the group that appeared as most envisioned Christ to be, white, long haired, bearded, thin, and very American in appearance, "That I am."

"The end of time has arrived!" The murmur began coursing its way through the religious leaders and rapture-hopefuls. "They are here to rapture us away from this cesspool of evil!"

"We come in peace," The one who had addressed himself as Jesu began, "and to bring peace. We come to bring you Heaven on Earth. An end to your sorrows."

"Come," Yam interjected, "and learn war no more. Learn to serve your fellows as you serve the Lord you God."

"Become princes of men," Yah seemed to smile at the phrase as he spoke it, "under us."

"Let us bow and give thanks," One of the religious leaders urged, "for the Lord has returned to put to death this world!"

A cheer rose above the religious collective present. a horrible, ignorant, blind cheer. As if they relished in an end they could not possibly know awaited them.

"We should learn from each other," one of the scientists offered, "you could teach us of new technologies. New methods of farming. New medicines."

"All in due time," Yam urged, "Now, we must meet with your leaders."

"I am the leader here," the president rudely pushed his way to the front with his cabal of criminals and the congress members who supported his corruption, "I rule this land."

"Then," Yam grinned darkly, "I shall start with you. Then, I will meet with those who would pray to us."

"Shall we go to the White House?" The president demanded. "Or shall we meet on your ship?"

"We shall go to your abode," Yah stated emotionless, "for now. Future meetings will take place upon our ships."

"As you wish," came the response.

The alien visitors were ushered into limos and sped away to the White House. The religious leaders, praising the lord, took their leave with their respective flocks. All who had gathered scattered until only the scientists remained.

As they studied the ship, the scientists seemed to suddenly realize that these visitors were not what they claimed. They were not gods. They weren't saviors.

"Dear God," One of the scientists muttered, "what have we done? What horror have we brought upon humanity?"

More aliens flooded from the ship and surrounded the scientists. A select few were lucky enough to escape, but the majority were taken captive. The subjugation of Earth had begun.

I WATCHED THE BROADCAST. I could see past the illusion being cast. I could see the aliens for what they were. Predators. Slavers.

I could not believe my eyes as I watched the scene. Though I could believe that the religious community was suddenly willing to give all in order to follow these aliens, and that our government (as corrupt as it was) was willing to meet peaceably with these monsters, I could not believe the initial response of the science community. Sure, these beings represented a chance to learn advanced technologies, but that was not why they came.

Though we had sought them out in friendship, they had come to enslave and to slaughter us. to eradicate us. Make us extinct.

Billy Monroe, Mac Stephens, and Larry White sat on the couch watching the telecast with me. Mac was so deep in shock that he couldn't utter a single word. Larry's mouth had dropped open at the precise moment the scientists had been taken.

"Can you believe that shit?" Came out of Billy's mouth every time something happened.

"Billy," I stated grimly, "I haven't believed much since the current administration got into office. This was something I have always feared might happen, but hoped I would never see."

"Whaddya mean?" He whipped his gaze to me, his face white as a ghost.

"Humanity is just not as intelligent as it believes itself to be," I sighed, rubbing my eyes, "even the scientific community isn't as smart as it wants to believe." I looked over at him. "Don't get me wrong, they're a hella smarter than most of us, just not smart enough to know better than to call out to the rest of the universe at this time. Not smart enough to realize that the other races out there might not be all that goddamn friendly."

"So I see," he muttered, still trying to grasp what I had just said, "whadda we do now?"

"Well," I took a deep breath as I began, "we begin looking for others like ourselves. Military. Civilian. Medical personnel. The scientists who escaped...as well as those who were not there for whatever reason.

"Then we begin looking for allies beyond this planet. Anything that can combat these fuckers. Anything that can destroy them.

"Then we try to convince the rest of the world that these visitors are not our saviors. They ain't 'God' or 'Christ'. We hafta convince people that these aliens are only wanting to enslave humanity."

"Aright," he nodded, coming out of his shock, "how do we do that?"

"I dunno," I shrugged, "I ain't never done the hero thing before. Never really wanted to."

"Guess we'll wing it," he stated.

"First thing we hafta do is snap Larry and Mac outta their shock," I admitted, "we'll need all four of us on this."

"Let's get started then," He averred, "it's gonna be a long affair."

We Come In Peace

Snapping Larry and Mac out of their shock proved more difficult than we thought. Neither wanted to believe what they had just seen, not that I blamed them. I couldn't.

Hell. *I* didn't even want to believe it. Yet, there it was.

I knew that the problem was bigger than the four of us. It was probably bigger than all those we might find to ally ourselves to. This was because none of us had been in the military.

I had grown up in one of those religions that now flocked to the aliens in the belief that they were God returning to reclaim what was his. They had taught, until I had long since left, that we were to be pacifists. We were not to fight the "world's" wars. We were to be witness to them and against the world itself.

We were taught a lot of bull shit. Including a running to a 'place of safety'. A sort of religious hiding place where we would wait out the war of 'Armageddon'–the war to end all wars. Looking back, it was all a bunch of lies based on misinterpretations meant to make a description of an internal battle into a physical event.

Now, man had lost that war. Both inwardly and outwardly. They had accepted an illusion for the truth and were about to pay for it.

Still, those of us fighting to free humanity would have need of just such a place. Some place the aliens could not find. Some place they could not survive.

But we would have to invent a way for us to survive. After all, even I knew that we would not be able to survive anything the aliens could not survive without some sort of personal life support. Yet, none of us were scientifically or imaginatively persuaded enough to dream up anything that elaborate.

"Lar," I stated, "can you check the local university to see if the professors in the science department are still free?"

"Sh-sure, man," He nodded, "why?"

"We need a system to get messages through to all within the science community who have still not been rounded up by the aliens," I began, "we need to gather them together into our own group."

"Why?" He inquired, still clueless as to what we were really doing.

"We sure as hell can't make personal life support systems ourselves," I gave him a sideways look, "we need science for that. technology is a part of science."

"Oh," he replied dumbly, "I see."

"Git started, man," I implored him, "we don't have time to waste!"

he scrambled to his feet shakily and went to complete the task I had sent him to do.

"Mac," I shook my other friend out of his stupor, "Your cousin still in the service?"

"Yup," he nodded.

"Go call him," I responded, "tell him to gather all the military he can. We'll need all we can get."

"Right away," he jumped up and disappeared.

"Now what?" Billy inquired.

"Now," I smiled grimly, "we wait."

"HOW WOULD WE GET AN S.O.S message out without the aliens picking up on it?" I inquired, looking at the astronomer who sat across from me.

"We don't," he shook his head, "at least, not with our current technology. It was, after all, a message that brought them. they will likely pick up anything we send from this point on."

"Can we encrypt in such a way that it would sound like gibberish or somethin'?" I pressed.

"Sure," he averred, "but it might seem that way to any we might want help from as well."

"Is there any way to make the alien communication ship go down just long enough to get a single message through?" I asked.

"Possibly," he nodded, "if someone could get close enough to it for a short time, just long enough to slip one message through, without getting caught."

"True," I frowned, "that is a problem. Getting close enough without being discovered and captured."

"Would an EMP work?" Mac inquired.

"It might," he nodded, "if we had one."

"We have the remnants of the military headed our way with vehicles and weapons," Mac responded, "not sure how well our weapons will work on the aliens, though."

"Bullets might wound them," he admitted, "and even kill them, but that is still unknown."

"Do they have any kind of body armor?" I queried.

"The soldiers seem to have a light armor," he stated, "though how effective it is is not known."

"So," Larry sat back presumptuously, "Jeff's theory about finding a place where they cannot survive as a sort of place of safety is the only sure fire way of defeating them."

"Yes," he replied, "and no. As far as a base is concerned, it is the only true way to stay safe, the idea of finding some place inhospitable. The only problem is that it would also be the end of us as well–unless we were to design a cross between armor and individual life support to counter the effect of our eventual base."

"Pressure suits with oxygen filtration," I smirked, "combined with impervious armor."

"Precisely," he grinned, "but we neither have the materials nor the manpower to design, let along build, such a thing."

"So," I looked away, "we return to the question of getting an S.O.S. out."

"Yes," he admitted, "we return to that question." He paused for a few minutes, as if in thought. "We'll attempt the EMP idea first. If it fails, we will search for another way."

"You think they are immune to Earth's viruses?" I looked up, an idea forming in my mind.

"There's no telling what kind of viruses they have been exposed to," he began, "but I am quite sure that they have not been exposed to those of our planet. We can always try a viral attack at some point. Good thinking." He slapped my back. "I'll make a scientist out of you yet."

"One step at a time, Doc," I grinned sheepishly, "one step at a time."

"One step at a time, Doc," I grinned sheepishly, "one step at a time."

The Disappearances

I had never seen an alien invasion movie that remotely resembled what was currently taking place. Not even the television series *V* came close. Most movies and television shows pictured aliens as either openly destructive, seeking to wipe out humanity in order to use the planet's core as fuel, or seductively deadly–seeing mankind as simply food. There seemed to be no in between.

And yet, in the movies, man is smart enough to see the aliens for what they were. Invaders. Predators.

Not one movie could have predicted the reaction our visitors received. around the world, the religious communities had been pulled in by the aliens and made to believe that they-the aliens-were the gods returning to lead man into the next age. Even the world's politicians and government leaders fell for the whole "God come to redeem man" act. Perhaps it was because of their greed that they fell so hard for it. Or, maybe, they were hoping for something that had been a lie all along.

Only those who had left the religious life behind saw through the illusion being cast. Many began fleeing from the capital cities as the extremely religious flocked to them. Those who fled began collecting in the outlying cities at first.

When alien influence began to spread, they retreated to the interior. Once there, they sought us out and joined with us. Many felt guilt as they could not reach their elderly family member and had to leave them behind. They felt as if they had sacrificed them. Left them to die.

Perhaps they had. But it had not been their choice. They'd had to leave quickly or become a slave themselves. Or a meal.

Even they realized that. Still guilt played upon them for a while until they had come to terms with it all. But those left behind would not be forgotten. They would become a part of our battle cry.

Amid this, the aliens and our government officials continued to televise updates on supposed peace accords. Every televised update lacked one human, though the number of aliens remained the same. Then, that person would reappear in the next update–though there was something very different about them. They were almost–robotic.

It had begun. The disappearances. First, the public officials. And the religious leaders. Then, those who had bowed to the aliens.

I studied the officials who returned to the televised updates closely, searching for something I could definitively claim as a change.At first, I could not find anything. And when I did, I was unsure that I had not imagined it.

"Am I imagining things?" I asked Dr. Hargrove. "Or does it look as if there is a headband around Representative Turley's head?"

"You're not imagining things," he responded, "and you can see the LEDs blink periodically from beneath his hair along the sides of his head."

"In other words," I began, "he has been enslaved."

"Yes," he agreed, "as have all who have returned to the telecasts." He turned to me. "We need to watch some of the Sunday broadcasts to see if the preachers and priests have found the same fate."

"I agree," I nodded, "though we will have to be careful. Never know what they will try over the airwaves."

"True," He averred, "and we have no idea what kind of subliminal tricks they might try."

Our ploy with the EMP had worked. We had been able to send at least three S.O.S. messages out into space, each describing our attackers and our plight. We could only hope that those who received the messages would be friendly, or at least a foe of our attackers, enough to come to our aid. WE HELD NO ILLUSIONS. It was likely that most alien races would be hostile. Perhaps even similar to our current invaders. But we had to try everything we had at our disposal to rid ourselves of our current invasion. Even if it meant inviting a second invasion.

I only hoped that the latter was not the case. I hoped that we found friendlies, not hostiles. We didn't need to become an opportunity for some other militant race.

We were desperate. We were running out of time. If we could not find allies, humanity would be destroyed.

"Don't Worry, Jeff," Dr. Hargrove assured me, "we'll find allies. Somewhere."

"I sure hope you're right," I sighed, exasperated, "not sure we can take these fuckers by ourselves."

"It is always darkest before the dawn," He smiled, "it always seems the most hopeless before we succeed."

"Yeh," I nodded and smiled sadly, "my grandpa always said that when things seemed hopeless."

"He was right, you know," he admonished.

"True," I chuckled nervously, "Things always resolve themselves."

"Of course," He nodded, "It is nature's way of resetting itself."

EVERY SINGLE LEADER had been subverted. Our public servants were no longer ours. Our leaders were now under the control of the aliens.

While wars between nations ceased, there was an unnatural feel to the whole process. Refugees were no longer turned back at what had been the borders of every country. Many disappeared, never to be seen again.

Those who remained fled from Europe, Asia, and Africa in search of some open coastal region in the eastern US where they could land. Some were even seeking entry to the west. And to the south.

What had been strong militaries were now reduced to small groups of resistance. Most supplied a defense for those seeking asylum as they fled. The tactic seemed effective enough, no matter how weak it seemed.

They slowly filtered into our little haven. The military collected in one area, the civilians in another.

"We're going to have to ask the military to begin training the civilians in warfare," I stated, matter-of-factly. "if we're to survive this invasion. there can no longer be any civilians. Not even I can remain a civilian."

"You're beginning to sound like that hero-type you claimed to never be," Billy chided smartly, "and you're damn good at it."

Changes

We began finding the bodies not long after Earth's remnants had collected in the Midwest and western US. The aliens held only the east coast at that point, and we held everything west of the Mississippi River. But the western US was all that they did not possess.

They had all of Eurasia, Africa, and Australia. They avoided Antarctica and the arctic regions since they could not survive the extreme cold. Beyond their intolerance of the cold, we knew nothing about them.

As I stated, we began finding the bodies shortly after those left had collected and begun to train to take back Earth. The discoveries started with the arrival of what I now realize was a slave sent to spy on us. The man looked somewhat normal, though he seemed to have a visor-like cover over his face that seemed to make his face seem pixelated but in HD.

You could see the line where the visor ended, along the cheeks. Oddly enough, the sides of his face, where the jaw was, did not move when his mouth in front did. I found this odd, as all normal humans' mouths moved as a single unit, not separately.

"Pin him down," I instructed one of the soldiers nearest me, "something about him is not right."

"Right, boss," he nodded and did as he had been instructed.

"I am going to try and remove this thing from his face," I stated, grabbing what I thought to be a face shield, "and try to free him from his slavery."

I gave the shield a sudden tug and the slave gave a loud, mortal shriek. There was the sudden sound of suction, then a loud pop. The unit I had taken hold of came loose without warning and I pulled the poor slave's face off, along with his brain. His head was now completely hollow.

I stood staring, shocked, at the hollowed out cavity that had been the poor man's head. his brain had been encased in a metal casing that had sheared it off at the base of the spine when I yanked on the unit covering his face.

I had never seen such a thing. The aliens had made humans into permanent slaves, surgically, by removing their facial structure and encasing the brain in a sort of tank where drugs kept them mindles. Their facial structure was then replaced by a sort of monitor where their original face was projected as if it were real.

They were kept fed through a system of intravenous tubes that carried food from some hidden packs within their torsos where a life support system also lay hidden. In reality, they were no longer human.

Of course, we would not discover the hidden life support or IV feeder source until our doctors dissected the poor man's remains. Such a horrible way to die, made into a techno-zombie. Neither alive nor dead.

Our tech people disassembled the slave's face to discover how it was constructed. They found that it was no mere television monitor, but a complex mechanism that also housed a small bomb big enough to blow just the unit and the attached brain. It kept the life support going. It kept the brain drugged.

I found the whole thing sickening. The slaves were not alive, at least not by nature's standards. They were walking dead people.

No mind. No will of their own. No future.

This had been the aliens' intent for all humanity. It had been the fate intended for all. Not just the handful who had suffered it.

Had the captured scientists suffered this fate? Or had they been the ones force to do this horrendously nightmarish deed? I hated to imagine either way.

THE FIRST BODY TURNED up shortly after I had destroyed the slave-spy. Like the slave that had entered our camp, its head was hollowed out, but the monitor was gone. Unlike the infiltrator, they had not been attacked by any within our sanctuary lands. Nor could anyone recollect seeing any other slaves. Or hearing explosions.

Had these slaves found a self-destruct switch? Had they committed suicide rather than continue living a meaningless life? Or had they been sacrificed?

I found it odd that there was no mess. The head, or the hollow portion, was still intact. And though the brain and the monitor were missing. Almost as if they had been pulled out as I had done to the spy.

The sight was horrible. I would have nightmares for months after. Had this been the fate the aliens had intended for all? To use, then kill?

I was sure that it had been. Slaves, after all, were only good until they were used up. Had these slaves been destroyed because they could no longer function as they should? Or had they been damaged?

We would find out that it was far less conspicuous. It was not any of those. It was a virus within the system, something planted by the human scientists as a way of causing the self-euthanasia of certain slaves who had been made against their will.

I would even witness such an event not too long after the fifth such body was found. I would be out on patrol with Billy and one of the Russian refugees when it would happen. It would change us forever.

"JEFF, LOOK!" BILLY had spotted it first and pointed to the struggling slave.

"Ho-ly shit!" I exclaimed, looking where he was pointing and spotting it. "What the hell is it doing?"

"Not sure," He returned, "but whatever it is, it ain't good."

"It's trying to pull its face off," Uri stated, looking through his binoculars, his thick Russian accent somewhat screwing with the words,"let me see if I can discover what he, er it, is saying." He held up the parabolic listening device he had been attentive enough to bring along. "No promises."

He had been smart enough to attach the device to a sound recorder as well. Billy quickly attached his video camera to the setup and we got both video and audio of the horrendous scene we were now watching.

"*Get out of my head!*" He was screaming in digital. "*I don't want you there!*"

"It's almost as if he has a battle going on inside his head," Billy whispered, "he is the first sentient, the first we have encountered who is aware that something is wrong anyway, we have seen. the other seemed to speak only what it was preprogrammed to say."

"*I said get* **out!!**" The poor man screamed.

We continued to watch as he tugged and pulled at the monitor, both sickened and entranced. He seemed to know that the monitor was the answer to his dilemma.

"*One more tug and I should be free of you...*" he grunted. "*Never wanted to be your slave! I was on to you from the very beginning. Now,* **out!**"

We watched in horror as he pulled the monitor free. The pop was loud enough for us to hear and pick up on the video. The monitor went flying, landing a few yards away. There was a pop when it exploded, and then, nothing.

A Stroke Of Luck

Though war was not yet upon us, we needed more information on how the aliens converted their slaves. We did not yet know whether all were transformed into the mech slaves we had just encountered, or whether there were different levels of slavery. But this was just the tip of what we did not know.

Did they use telepathy? Could they sense us near? What did they look like behind the illusion? Exactly *what* could kill them, if anything?

If they were telepathic, could tinfoil shield our thoughts from them? Or was that ineffective? What about military helmets?

Our opportunity came when one of the alien soldiers strayed into our territory and became so entangled within our nets that he/it could not free itself.

Free me, it tried to command one of the soldiers in my patrol, *free me, slave.*

"I am not your slave," he responded, "I take orders only from Jeff and he has not commanded me to release you."

Release me and your reward will be great, it promised in a lie.

"Nothing doing," the soldier returned.

Show me this Jeff, it demanded, *perhaps it will see the need to release me.*

"I doubt that, alien," I smirked, "I am Jeff."

I see nothing where the voice came from, it was now in a panic, *what trickery is this?*

It suddenly dawned on us that I did not exist to the aliens. I smiled.

"No trickery," I began, taunting, "I am God of this world. And I lead these men in their mission to clear your kind from Earth."

But how can you not be seen? It begged.

"Cage it," I commanded my patrol, ignoring the alien's frantic question, "we'll take it to base. radio ahead and tell the doctors to have a manually operated restraint table ready. we're going to interrogate this alien and take vitals to see if we can defeat them easily."

I knew that my decision was likely declaring war upon the aliens, but I didn't care as long as we could gather vital information from them. Their weaknesses. Their physiology. The makeup of their armor. Why some of us existed to them while others did not.

I watched as three of my soldiers wrapped the alien so that it could no longer beg or plead for its release. I got the feeling that they were also trying to ensure that it could not attempt to use any mental powers against them as we transported it back to base. I couldn't blame them.

One took a syringe and loaded it with a tranquilizer. Surprisingly, he found a weak spot in the alien's armor and sedated the pittiful being. This made it easier for the other two soldiers to bind the limp alien to a makeshift stretcher so that it could be transported.

After untangling it from the netting-once it was sedated and unable to attack-and securing it to the stretcher, we began our patrol again. This time, we headed back to camp. The sooner we got the captive back to the docs, the sooner we could pry answers from it.

"ASK IT WHY IT CANNOT see me," I instructed.

"Why can't you see Jeff?" The doctor demanded.

You humans, it began, *or most of you, are easy for us to see. Mentally, you are bright beacons to us. And though some are dim, most are bright lights. It depends on your level of intelligence. That is how we see you. your psy-waves.*

As with all races, there are also some who do not appear to us. Some races have learned to block us from seeing them. Others are naturally endowed with such an ability. While we can hear them, physically, we cannot see them. This makes them deadly to us since they do not psychically exist to us.

"How do we kill your kind?" I asked.

Find the weaknesses in our armor, it began, *or find a disease that you are immune to that we are not.*

"Can we see through your illusions?" I pressed.

"Yes," it nodded, *with this...though a null-that's what we call those we cannot see-might also be able to see us as we truly are.*

It handed the doctor a visor of sorts.

"Then," I nodded, "I could possibly see your leaders as they truly are without the visor?"

"Yes, it averred, *you are a threat to all of us. Unseen. A voice without an origin. The perfect assassin.*

"Will your own weapons work against you?" I pushed.

"*Yes,* it weakly nodded, *if you are successful enough to steal samples.* it paused. *May I inquire what you injected into me?*

"A tranquilizer," I began, "we sedated you so we could safely transport you. Why?"

"*It is slowly killing me,* it replied, *its chemical makeup is unknown to my race. Please, I beg you, end my misery. I can no longer detect any of you because of the poison.*

I nodded to the scientist, who euthanized the alien.

"Study what you can of his anatomy before he decomposes too much," I instructed, "then disassemble his armor and study it in hopes of creating something similar for us." I looked around at all present. "we know two things. First, viruses and other diseases will kill them as will earthly medicinal chemicals. These natural weapons we can use to our advantage.

"Secondly, their own weapons will kill them. Which gives us hope."

"Sir," a soldier interrupted, "we also know that they cannot see you or others."

"Good," I smiled, "you *were* listening."

I HAD OPTED TO GO ON this first scouting mission alone. No need to jeopardize anyone else. After all, the aliens could not see me. I did not exist to them.

We all knew that war was inevitable. Once the alien soldier did not return, its superiors would search for it. when it could not be found, they would realize that it had been taken hostage. This would cause them to declare war.

I hoped that I could steal some of the alien weapons before that happened. We needed to be prepared. Hell. We needed all the help we could get.

I Spy With My Eye

I was transported to an abandoned airport near the alien craft. There, I disembarked the helicopter and began recon activity. Though I had never been a spy, or even a military scout, I had the advantage. I did not exist to the aliens.

From the airport, I took to the shadows and headed for the alien craft. The city was empty. Dead.

Not a soul moved in the houses, apartments, or shops. Food sat, untouched, upon store shelves. Guns and ammo sat in the sporting goods department of some. It was almost as if they were waiting for someone to come and pick them up.

I figured that most of the population was now slave labor. Some may have joined me long ago, but most were probably enslaved. I had no hopes of finding any free souls here. Not in the capital. Not here on the east coast.

I approached the alien craft warily. It looked nothing like the saucers that Hollywood had taken from urban legend and made mythical. Nor was it the supposed orb-shaped or cigar-shaped ships often described by supposed abductees.

Instead, it looked like a city on a saucer, but with a jagged spike on the bottom that served as the entry and exit from the craft. Had I been a betting man, I would have bet that the craft had been built around sections, cities, from their home planet. their appearance seemed to be such that such thoughts were easy to arrive at.

I chuckled to myself. Flat Earthers would have been in Heaven with this craft. It epitomized their ideas where Earth was concerned.

I pulled myself out of my thoughts and began searching for an alternate way into the craft. Some port. Some vent.

I found an air duct just above the main entrance and crawled in. I narrowly escaped discovery as an alien soldier emerged from the main entry shortly after I replaced the vent grate. I began to follow the ducting, believing it would take me where I wanted to go.

It would, but I would also witness things I would have nightmares from for days to come. I would also hear things that caused the pieces of the puzzle to fall into place.

I heard voices ahead of me. The president. The Vice President. Several congressmen and women. The new alien masters.

Though I could not make out what was being said, I knew I had to listen in once I arrived to where they were. I hit the record button on my recorder and hoped I had enough tape to ensure a capture of all that was said.

I HALTED ABOVE THE conference room. Below, what had been the president and his cabinet stood, mind control bands around their heads. Though they had been no more than useful idiots in life, I now felt a tinge of pity for them. Now, they no longer functioned freely.

Resistance to our coming has been rather...surprising, considering the primitiveness of your race, I heard the mental voice of one of the alien leaders state, *those who resist have apparently taken one of my soldiers captive. No matter. It will be easy to destroy them."*

"They will fall to your will, oh master," I heard the empty voice of the president state.

Of course they will, hissed the one that had claimed to be Jesus, *or they will die.*

"They will see reason," the Vice President said, mindlessly agreeing with the president.

And if they do not? Yah demanded.

"Then they are doomed," stated one of the now enslaved senators.

You will pass laws commanding them to surrender and come in, Yam commanded, *You will command them to lay down their weapons.*

"As you wish, master," Came the unified response.

"The president will urge them to come in as you begin making it illegal to resist us, Yam demanded.

"Your wish is my command," the president replied.

As he spoke, the president looked up where I was hidden. Did he sense my presence? Or had the action been reactionary?

I would not, I decided, stick around long enough to find out. I muffled the sound of me turning off the recorder and swiftly moved past the vent I had been watching through. after I rounded a bend and was out of view, I heard an alien lift the grate where I had been

"Bah! I heard Yah's muffled voice exclaim. *There must be a small glitch in the mindbender halo that causes them to look up.*

"Nothing, then? I heard Jesu inquire.

"Not a whisper of a scent, Yah informed his fellow leader.

I STOPPED AT A GRATE above what looked like a laboratory. Below, I could see a human with wires coming out of every conceivable pore and hole. The alien 'doctors' were performing something, but I could not tell what it was. Turning on my video feed, I allowed the data to collect.

They could analyze what was taking place once I got safely back to base. The poor man's screams did not take long to affect me. No one deserved to suffer like that. No one.

Yet, I could do nothing to end his misery. Not if I wished to remain unseen. Thus, I moved on.

The third port overlooked the lab where the 'monitor' slaves were made. I watched as human scientists removed the front of a "devotee's" skull, face and all. one of the scientists glanced up and saw me, though did not give a visible sign for fear of giving me away. But I had seen his look of recognition, though as brief as it was, before he quickly looked back at what he was doing.

he had given me a sign, but not the aliens. He had been pleading. Begging.

And yet, he knew that I could do nothing. Nor could he give away the fact that I was aboard and spying. He could only return to what he was doing, no matter how horrifying.

I moved on and found the armory. here, I finally dropped into the room. I scouted the armory and made sure I was alone. Undetected.

Then, I began gathering weapons. As I did so, I wondered if the aliens would miss one of their attack vessels. Or if I could even fly it.

I decided I would try. We needed something to help us design our own defensive warships. Something that would give us an edge.

I loaded my ill gotten gains into one of the flying vessels, then sought the cockpit. I started the engine. It was so quiet! As I shot out of the bay opening, several alien soldiers flooded the armory and began shooting at my escaping ship.

Stolen Gems

I had been fortunate enough to steal ten sets of the alien armor as well as a dozen guns and assorted other weapons. The warcraft I had also stolen would offer an opportunity for the scientists to study and replicate alien technology. The video and audio gave us plenty to observe, but only the audio gave us anything definitive.

For instance, we knew that they planned to make us outlaws. Enemies of the state. And they believed we were dumb enough to fall for their trap.

They wanted us to give in without a fight. Become their slaves willingly. Something that was never going to happen.

"You did good, Jeff," the head of our intel division asserted, "you got us audio of what they are planning."

"I felt it was necessary," I averred, "important. Something just told me to hit record at that point in time."

"And well you did," She nodded, "You've saved us all."

"All in a day's work," I smiled.

"Now," she admonished, "don't get cocky. We don't want you making a mistake and getting caught."

"So," I began, "What's next?"

"First," she started, "we allow the science and technology department to study the weapons and armor you brought us to see if they can replicate them. Same with the warcraft you stole. Once they are able to, we wait until they can build you both.

Then, we send you out on more recon missions since you are the only one thay seem to not see."

"And the video of that poor man?" I inquired.

"we will study it to see what is happening," she sat back, "then, we will run over it with you. We may need you to—plant a few bugs for us."

"Not hard to do," I shrugged, "as long as I don't have to go and blend in."

"No," she smiled, "nothing like that. More....ductwork, though."

"I see," I nodded, "stealth work."

"pretty much," she giggled, "but no theft."

"See if Tech can design a sniper rifle using the alien guns," I suggested, "when I have to take on out, I don't want them to see it coming."

"Will do," she promised, "but for now, you will have a crossbow with special bolts."

"Intriguing," I uttered, "able to penetrate their armor?"

"of course," she winked, "and some will carry certain viruses and infectious bacteria in tranq-dart configuration."

"Chemical warfare," I mused.

"Yes," She admitted, "everything from sarin and anthrax to the plague and typhoid."

"That's quite a wide range of infectious diseases," I remarked.

"Perhaps they will spread it through their own community. And their slaves," she suggested, "though there is a slight risk of it spreading back to us."

"As always," I nodded.

CHEYENNE MOUNTAIN BECAME our temporary home. As a bunker, it was somewhat safer than our other options at this point.

We were met by the commander of NORAD.

"You're trespassing on US military property," He warned.

"There is no US military," I responded, "and no nations of the world. There is just us and you. We represent what is left of the world population."

"What the fuck happened out there?" He demanded.

"Our governments were taken over by the aliens," I informed him, "there is no longer a president, VP, or Congress. Even the Supreme Court is gone. All are now under the control of the aliens."

"And the military?" He was hesitant.

"Those who were near the ship are either prisoners or enslaved," I answered, "Those still on the bases retreated to our location in Iowa and regrouped. It was upon their suggestion that we headed here for safety."

"Damn," he breathed, "I was wondering why there had been no word from Washington."

"The religious leaders of the world gave up without a fight," I stated, almost as if I had read his thoughts, "and they bowed in reverence to the illusion cast by the invaders."

"Fucking idiots," he scowled.

"We have intel that they will be passing laws," our intel chief began, joining us, "to coax all resistance in peaceably. They will be outlawing resistance."

"The hell they will," he seethed, "who collected the intel?"

"I did, sir," I responded, "since I don't exist to them, I can slip aboard their ship. I also stole some of their weapons and armor. And a warcraft."

"Then," he smiled, "I see no reason why you shouldn't remain our chief spy."

"It'll be an honor, sir," I saluted.

"For Christsakes!" He exclaimed, slurring Christ and sakes into a single word. "At ease, soldier."

"We'll be sending him back in as soon as Tech is finished examining and replicating the alien technologies, adapting them for human use."

"Good, good," he nodded, "and what will his mission be?"

"To plant a video and audio bug above both the meeting room he recorded the discussions on trying to coax us in over and above the labs he brought video feed from."

"The purpose?" He was curious.

"We want to get a closer look at the headbands on the leaders," She averred, "for one. And for another, we wish to learn exactly what was going on in those laboratories."

"Very good," he nodded, "we need to collect all the intel data we can."

"I suggest that you put out a coded message for all military still out to collect here," I advised.

"I agree," he smiled, "and will do so immediately. We'll try to connect up with Ghost Lake, Groom Lake, and a few other unmarked bases."

He ushered us inside.

"Unfortunately," he began, "we aren't designed to house so many people. We're only capable of handling 800. Not..." He gestured to our group.

"We understand that," our intel chief averred, "but, perhaps, we can...expand the facility. Eventually."

"We were thinking," he nodded, "that we should go deeper and run tunnels and even, perhaps, creating a city under the mountain."

"We might even be able to hide the city under the mountain range itself," one of the men in our group stepped forward, "a few of us are former miners, mudjackers, and sandhogs. I think some of us could even secret the equipment west from the coast."

"Once enough of a military presence is here," the general looked at him, "we will see to that mission. You will need cover."

Back Into Hell

I was flown to the abandoned airport near Washington, DC again. This time, I was armed with the crossbow and two wireless bugs and several relays. The bugs were to be planted in the air ducts of the alien ship. The relays were meant to be attached to the now idle cell towers that dotted the landscape in between.

I knew that my return to base would be slow, but I didn't care. Perhaps I could glom onto a semi, trailer and all, and abscond with the food that was now sitting abandoned in the stores that lay on my path home. I kind of wished that I had been allowed an assistant so he could glom onto a fuel truck, but I understood why they refused to take the chance.

We knew absolutely nothing about the aliens. How they gained control of their human supplicants. How they detected their victims.

All we knew was that they could not sense me. I did not exist to them. I could slip in on them without warning and leave behind whatever I was asked to leave.

It made me the perfect spy. The perfect thief. And the perfect assassin.

I took aim at the guard the aliens had left to deter me from doing my job. rather than use a large bolt, I opted for the small dart gun on my arm.

the dart hit its target and injected the virus, then disappeared. Perfect hit. The alien guard slapped the back of its neck.

I wondered how the malaria parasite would affect the alien. How quick would it take? What symptoms would be the first to develop, if any? Would it spread through the collective as it did with humans? Or would it ride their psionic connection?

I watched as the alien suddenly collapsed without warning. Interesting. I had not seen that coming.

I slipped into the ductwork of the ship unseen. Unsensed. Unhampered.

It would take time for them to discover their comrade. By then, I would be gone and the bugs would be planted. Hell. I would probably be to my next destination.

I quietly made my way to the conference room. I had but one mission here. I didn't need any weapons. I only had to plant the bugs.

I was soundless as I went. No need to alert them to my presence. No need to set off alarms.

I smiled. So far, so good. I corrected myself. No need to get cocky. Being cocky caused mistakes. Big mistakes.

I SLID OUT OF THE DUCTWORK on the other side of the ship. Both bugs were now in place and two aliens had succumbed to two different illnesses. I had been very effective.

I had successfully completed another mission. The aliens would never know that I had been there. Not unless they looked at the backs of their soldiers' necks.

Did they have necks? What did they actually look like? would our cameras catch them as they were? Or as they appeared?

I would have to wait for those answers. Now, I had to make it to the first tower and attach the relay transponder. To do that, I would have to find a car or some automobile.

I was also getting hungry. I hadn't eaten since I left the base. That had been ten hours ago.

As I slipped from shadow to shadow, I wondered how long it would take for the aliens to program a human to betray me. To help them see me. So far, I had been lucky and they suspected nothing.

But that would come to an end once they realized that I could assassinate them without being detected. I hoped they wouldn't even try. I hoped that they refused to believe that their comrades had been killed by a human agent.

I hoped that they would believe that their soldiers had accidentally uncovered an old human weapon, some canister of gas, and had loosed whatever had been inside trying to discover what it was. Still, I knew better. Perhaps they might initially come to that conclusion, but they would figure it out at some point.

Then I would be a sitting duck. I would have to hide. I would no longer be able to spy for my own.

It could possibly spur them into finding a cure or vaccine compatible with their physiologies. Or maybe to create a better armor. One I would not be able to find the weakness of.

For now, The mission had been a success. I had proven that they were susceptible to human diseases. I had planted the bugs.

I ARRIVED AT THE LAST tower and climbed to the top. It was after dark and I wanted to be done. I had spent six days on the road in a truck with two trailers. One was filled with diesel, the other was filled with food.

I had done well. Rather than use the fuel in the tanker, I stopped regularly and siphoned off gas from abandoned tanks at stations. Perhaps I would make more trips to gather more fuel. I didn't know.

That was up to my superiors. All missions were. As long as I didn't have to lead, I was happy following orders.

The road headed toward base was a lonely one. Empty. I could remember when the interstate was packed with cars and trucks.

But here we were. A third of the population had fallen into darkness. We were what was left.

We outnumbered them, sure. But we were still without weapons that could kill them outright. Bioweapons didn't count.

They were dirty. Dangerous. Potentially lethal to us as well.

Their use had to be limited. We could never use them wholesale. It was too dangerous.

BUt what about nukes? We had precision nukes. One that could hit a predesignated target with a 90% accuracy. We also had 'dirty' bombs. But how effective would they be?

I placed the relay at the top of the tower, then climbed down. This part of my mission was now complete as well. I went to the truck and climbed in.

Time to head for base. Time to head for bed. And safety.

Storm On The Horizon

"See these links here?" The scientist who had done the video analysis pointed at the enlarged frame to a couple thin silver lines running from the halo-like headband into the president's head. "I believe this is how the aliens control their non transformed slaves, the ones that are still living and breathing in the conventional sense."

"What would happen if we clipped those links?" The general inquired.

"There's no telling," the scientist admitted, "perhaps nothing. Or maybe death. We have no clue what preventative measures have been taken to keep removal of the halo from taking place. There may not be any. Or...there may be such an intricate preventative measure that we would risk detonating some hidden explosive that would destroy everything within a fifty foot perimeter."

"Then," the general understood the scientist's meaning, "death is the most merciful measure should we have a chance to save these poor souls."

"Affirmative," The scientist nodded.

"Alright," the general sat back, "continue with the next bit analyzed."

"We also analyzed the video of the laboratory," the scientist continued, "and though we were relieved to find that this was not the lab where the mindless slaves are made, we found that something much more horrible takes place in that lab. Something that transforms, twists, the individual subjected to the tortures they put captives through into something far more dangerous.

"As we watched, a captive human was hooked to wires and tubes and energies run through him. As these energies were run through him, something else was being done. Upon closer inspection, we realized that one of the aliens was being spliced into the captive. These aliens are a kind of cosmic parasite that feeds upon other races of beings. We, in essence, were intended as their food.

"But while the alien feasts upon its host," he started the enlarged video so that we were now watching what he was describing, "it uses its host as a way to travel and fight. They are, after all, fairly defenseless when not feeding. And they are far from human in appearance."

"Can they infect a human without the aid of the energies?" The general pressed.

"If what we witnessed was accurate, they have to be introduced through the tubing," the scientist responded, shaking his head, "perhaps at a larval stage. Sort of how a mosquito infects us with malaria."

"So," the general surmised, "they are nothing more than a giant germ."

"Yes," the scientist nodded, "for the most part...though they are far more intelligent than your run of the mill virus or bacteria. or even your average nematode."

"Can we find a vaccine or cure for them?" The general insisted.

"We are working on that," the scientist confirmed, "using the dead alien we captured."

"What is your timetable on such a thing?" The general asked.

"Weeks," the scientist affirmed, "maybe a couple months."

"Make it your number one priority," the general commanded.

"Yes sir," the scientist nodded.

"How are the weapons coming?" He asked.

"We have successfully replicated their rifles," a weapons tech confirmed.

"And the warcraft?" He pressed.

"It's proving to be a bit more complex," the tech admitted.

"any idea on when a replicated one will be ready for testing?" He was not happy.

"Two to three weeks," the tech nervously replied.

"Make it in two," he ordered, "we can perfect after the first tests are complete." He turned to me. "I need you to go back in and plant more bugs. Find other vents. See where they all lead. See if you can find the lab where the techno-zombies are created. We need to know how they do it. And how to stop them."

"Yes, sir," I saluted, "when do you want this done?"

"Immediately," he frowned.

"Consider it done," I saluted again.

"How is the armor coming?" He turned his attention to other issues and away from me.

"Jeff's armor is ready to be tested," The weapons tech averred, "as soon as he wishes to test it."

"I will test it out this round of recon," I offered, "I am also willing to test the other weapons as well."

"Good," the general smiled, "if the weapons work well, and without much difficulty, we'll expect enough to be made to equip all who are currently here in camp."

I SUITED UP. THE ARMOR was tight, but surprisingly light. though tight, it allowed for a great range of motion. The alien rifle snapped into place on the back as if by magnets and yet, was easily accessed when needed. the pistol snapped on the hip for quick access.

Something told me that the technology had not originated with our new invaders, but had been adopted by them when they had destroyed the original owners. Just seemed like a thing an intelligent parasite would do. Steal alien technologies.

After all, man was sometimes just as parasitic. We tended to steal things from others and call it our own as well. And we were a race of beings. Not a walking bacteria.

Once I was all suited up, I boarded the plane. I was ready to go in. I was ready to do what I had been asked to do.

But this time, I was armed with their weapons and was protected by their armor. This time, I was testing their technologies against them if I needed to. And I hoped I did.

"What's our destination?" I asked the pilot.

"The aliens have expanded their zone," she began, "so I cannot drop you at the airport where we dropped you the last two times. I can't get you anywhere near the ship now."

"What does this mean?" I queried.

"I have to drop you at the abandoned airport in Canton," She responded, "and you will have to journey the rest of the way either on foot or by stolen automobile."

"Ah," I smiled at her, "I get to hotwire a ride. Hope someone left their Harley so I can travel in style."

"Meet me back at the Canton airport in four days' time," she admonished, "and we'll head back to HQ."

"Will do," I replied.

What Horrors Lay Beyond Our Vision

I'd had no trouble getting in and back out of the alien ship. I'd had no problem placing the bugs where they could view all that went on. I'd had no problem making the rendez vous on time.

The new video surveillance was riding the same relays as the rest. That meant that I had no relays to set up. No stops to make.

I had not been worried. I knew the vents in and out of the ship like the back of my hand. I knew the aliens' habits.

I also knew how not to get caught. But then, the aliens could not sense me. I did not exist to the aliens.

I had also sensed that their slaves could not sense me either. Not once had a captive enslaved politician looked up where I was. Not once had an infected captive looked where I hid.

I had the advantage. If I did not exist, they could not combat me. They could not track me.

Not so much with my contacts. Or my drivers. They had to remain far enough away that the aliens could not sense them.

This made my trek to the rendez vous sites long and hazardous. Not because of the aliens, but because of the animals left without owners. And the wildlife that had already existed.

I killed any alien scout I caught away from the ship. I killed any slave I found wandering out of their zone. I took samples from both.

I hoped that the aliens would never find the bugs. They didn't need to know that we had been spying on them. Nor did they need to know that we had stolen some of their weapons.

If they found any of those things, we were as good as dead. As it was, we had no allies. Our hopes of defeating them was almost nil.

SCREAMING FILLED THE briefing room as we watched, for the first time, how the aliens created their mindless slaves. We watched as the acolyte was strapped to a surgical table, begging for mercy from the alien they saw as an emissary of their God. To our horror, we watched as the subject was not anesthetized before their face was carved from their skull and the frontal pieces of the skull was surgically formed in a dish shape within the now open skull. We watched as they encased the victim's brain in a shell where we were sure a mass of probes punctured it so that drugs could be pumped in freely to create a zombie.

This brain casing was slipped into a hole in the back of the face-shaped monitor as it was slipped into the fleshy pocket that had been made for it. When the procedure was complete, the monitor came on and the victim's face appeared, eyes now blank and empty.

"Ho-ly shit!" The general exclaimed. "That was the sickest thing I have ever witnessed and I have seen a *lot* of sick shit!"

"What we *do* know," one of the scientists began, "is that the brain casing is designed to clip the spinal cord if the monitor is removed. we also know that the casing includes a built into it so that nothing is left intact. We assume that this is to prevent any data important to the aliens and their operation from being retrieved."

"In other words," the general nodded, "they destroy the black box rather than risk whatever it has recorded from being downloaded."

"Precisely," the scientist averred, "which would make it almost impossible to capture one of these slaves to download any information."

"There is no hidden releases that we are overlooking?" The general pressed.

"We have been unsuccessful at capturing one to find out," the scientist responded, "the last one detonated itself."

"We better figure something out soon," The general scowled, "because the aliens are building for war."

"Perhaps," The scientist replied, "more surveillance will reveal some of the answers to some of the questions we have."

"Better be soon," the general warned, "because once the battle begins it'll be too late."

"WE'RE NOT SENDING YOU out for a while," The general stated, "we're gonna let you lay low. Don't need to unnecessarily run the risk of you getting caught."

"I understand," I nodded.

"Do you?" He flashed me a look of bewilderment. "Or are you just agreeing with me?"

"A little of both, sir," I smiled slyly, "I understand that I run the risk of discovery every time I go in. I understand that my discovery would lead to my capture. It is what keeps me so cautious when I go in."

"The assassination of the aliens guarding your last insertion point put you close to discovery. I understand that it was a necessary risk, but you cut it a bit close."

"I'm sorry about that, sir," I apologized, "it won't happen again."

"The problem is that you cannot prevent the inevitability of having to destroy or assassinate," he sat back, "but we can pull you back and hide you for a while. We know that, though you have the advantage, that doesn't mean that the aliens won't soon find a way to sense you."

"True," I nodded, "I am well aware of that."

And well you should be," He averred, "if you did not, you would become reckless. A liability."

"We wouldn't want that," I smiled knowingly, "would we, sir?"

"No we would not," He agreed, "not where you are concerned. You know the most about operations here. After all, you were integral in their formation."

"Here's hoping that the aliens remain clueless," I stated, "until it is too late."

"Agreed," he nodded, "though I sincerely hope that they never get a clue at all."

"Same here," I admitted, "I want to destroy them before they have a chance to gain too much of a foothold here."

"You and I both, soldier," he chuckled, "you and I both."
"I'll head to barracks now," I began, "if we are done."
"I'm finished," he smiled, "you're dismissed."

Last Days Of Peace

Over the successive days, we learned that we would never see the aliens as they truly were. Without a host body, they were defenseless. Without a host, they died quickly.

The soldiers were not their true image either. Rather, these poor sots were infected members of other races...most from the race that had originally created the armor. Most, when ensnared in our netting, would beg for death rather than suffer at the mercy of the being within them. The general soon ordered that we observe their wishes.

The order only came after we extracted vital information from the last live capture we made.

"What do these aliens thrive on?" The general demanded.

"Hate, greed, all the negative aspects of a civilization," the captive responded, "they appeal to the religions, the purists, and politically corrupt. Anyone who has not been corrupted does not exist to them. Those who are less evil will seem as ghosts or shadows to them and go largely unnoticed.

"Empty your hearts, I implore you, of hate and greed. Embrace knowledge and wisdom, ridding yourselves of the ignorance that breeds the negative traits. It is the only way to defeat them."

"Even our hate for them?" He pressed.

"Yes," it gasped, "rid yourself even of the hate you hold for the invader. Love is the answer."

"That's a tall order," he sighed, "but it is not impossible."

"Please," it gasped, "kill me. See it not as killing an enemy, but as having mercy upon a penitent being."

"Where might we find the being within you?" He asked. "We wish to see what the true alien looks like."

"It has been growing inside me for centuries," It whispered, "and is wrapped around my spinal cord. It has complete control of my body, but not my mind."

"Consider your wish granted," the general replied, then nodded to a scientist.

"Thank you," it whispered, a tear in its alien eye.

"It is the least we can do for you," he averred, then turned and issued the order to the scientist, "make it quick and painless. And when you dissect to find the alien within, be sure to place the corpse in a glass containment pod and do the dissection remotely."

"Yes, sir," the scientist nodded.

The alien died quickly and painlessly, an injection of poison administered so as not to destroy the alien within. At least, they hoped that the poison wouldn't destroy the alien within. There was no telling.

"CAREFUL," THE LEAD scientist advised, "careful. We don't need this thing loose in here. The containment pod must remain our safety buffer."

The incision was made carefully and the outer alien stripped slowly from the invader. I observed from a safe distance. It was hard to imagine that there was a world where viruses and bacteria had advanced to a multicellular semi sentient level, but here was one such evolutionary predator.

The host had lost all nervous structure, the parasitic alien replacing it. The revelation was sickening. No spine. No Nerve branches. Just a brain kept alive so that the host could remain living.

This was what the aliens had in store for most of their acolytes. A living death. Zombification without losing their own consciousness. Loss of control over their own bodies but not their minds.

Horrible. Maddening. Unimaginably sad and painful.

I wondered what happened should the host refuse to follow commands. were they injected with some sort of chemical to put them in a haze? Or *could* they even fight it?

I didn't want to really know. I could not imagine living with one of these parasites inside me. And yet, I wanted to know just how sentient these parasites really were.

Had they grown in intelligence with each successive race preyed upon? Or was the sentience an illusion? Something used as a ploy to gain trust?

The more we learned about our new foe, the more we found that we didn't know or understand. The more we realized just how primitive we really were. And the least civilized.

"HAVE WE HAD ANY ANSWER from our SOS?" I asked.

"Not yet," the general shook his head, "but we're not giving up yet. We do know that it got through. We also know that it did not call any more of these things. Apparently, this is all there is."

"That we know of," I grimaced.

"If we could discover their origin," he sighed, "we could bomb the planet with whatever vaccine we discover and kill them out."

"Always worth hoping, sir," I averred, "but not likely. Not unless the race originally infected comes to our aid."

"True," he nodded, "and there ain't no telling whether any of those survived."

"Precisely," I smiled sadly.

"We can hope, though," He suggested.

"nothing wrong with that," I shrugged, "rebellions are based on hope."

"Is that what you are calling this?" He was amused. "A rebellion?"

"Yes," I admitted, "sort of. They have usurped control. We are revolting to return control to us."

"Never looked at it that way," He raised an eyebrow, "but now that you mention it, you're right."

"We have a revolution to win, sir," I smiled.

"I agree," He chuckled.

"Afterwards," I continued, "we will have to address the problems that made this all too possible."

"The science or what?" He was unsure.

"No," I corrected, "the spirituality, or lack thereof, within our religious institutions."

"Pretty sure this has been the death of those," He opined.

"You could be right," I agreed, "but in case it isn't, we will need to address the problems within those institutions."

"After this," He snorted, "I'd be for shutting them down completely."

"We'll have to wait and see," I offered, "and go from whatever is left."

"True," he grinned, "may not be anything left at all."

"My thoughts exactly," I smiled sadly, "but I will reserve final judgment until the end."

"Good idea," he agreed.

We grew silent as the dissection of the alien parasite began. We both knew that this was likely one of the last peaceful days we would have. War was inevitable.

An Unexpected Ally

The parasitic alien had spread through thirty-six races with ease. The resistant members of each race had been pushed slowly from their planets and their systems by the invaders and had sought to save each successive race from the same fate. These races all lives within a few light years from one another and had been allies. Each fell, with ease, to the parasites.

Unlike the human race, the races before were easily infected...in much the same way humans can get such parasites as tapeworms or malaria. Some were merely bitten by an infected indigenous insect akin to Earth's mosquito or they merely stepped on a pile of dung that had the alien larvae in it and the larvae burrowed into them. The end result was the same. infection and growth.

But unlike Hollywood's blockbusters, there was no dramatic bursting open of chests or internal gestation that made an overtly external threat. The larva simply latched itself onto the nervous system of the host and took over all motor functions. The action turned the poor host into an unwilling participant in what the growing larva was doing. IN essence, they became unwilling soldiers, though still conscious enough to realize that they were helpless to do anything, in the parasitic alien invasion.

These unwilling soldiers were used to round up more victims. Or to kill those who rejected the parasitic aliens as their overlords. or to punish the mindless slaves.

But humanity proved to be more difficult. Infection had to be aided. Incubation had to be forced.

Otherwise, the parasite was expelled and the human was left useless or dead. Thus, incubation and infestation became a form of torture demanded of the new 'Messiah' and his fellow 'Elohim', something these imposters demanded of their worshipers. In return, they promised heaven, paradise, or whatever the worshiper believed in.

It was the remnants of these thirty-six alien races that first contacted us. But they would not be the most unexpected ally. Nor would they be the only allies.

There would be many, many more that would join our fight. Some would come at the beginning, others would join in later. All would become dear allies.

And I would negotiate all the treaties. All the alliances. Every contract.

I would create new trade partners. With every new treaty, a new chance to learn would present itself. New goods, new weapons, new types of armor would also be found.

But at the moment, thirty-seven allies were enough to get things started. Thirty-six had been at war with the parasite since a time long before humanity ever existed. The thirty-seventh had long since evolved beyond the sight of the parasite.

Perhaps they jall had something to teach mankind. Something humanity had yet to experience. Something that would make evolving a bit easier.

"I HEAR YOU ARE IN NEED of allies," the being before me stated through some sort of translator device.

"Yes," I nodded, "we have...been overrun by a extraterrestrial parasite."

"We call them the 'feasters," he/it smiled coldly, "As they eat nearly every being that exhibits negativity. Hate. Fear. Greed.

"Odd that they come to feast on a race so young as yours. They generally feast upon races that are nearing their end in this realm. Your race is no more than three billion years old. At the most."

"Then," I gave a puzzled look, "a race nearing its end would be...?"

"Trillions of years old," it stated, "quadrillions of years old. And still lacking enough empathy to evolve."

"And these 'feasters," I began, "they avoid those beings that are beginning to evolve?"

"They cannot see those who are beginning to evolve," it corrected, "they are drawn to negative traits. Not to positive results."

"Why can't they see me?" I pressed.

"Because," it smiled again, "you are in a sort of chrysalis, figuratively speaking, as you are beginning to evolve past what the rest of your race has stubbornly held tight to."

"Meaning?" I was confused.

"Meaning that you have cast away many of the negative traits," it grinned, "like hate, fear, ignorance, and greed-your basic love of self baggage-and so have risen above all the rest. Oddly enough, you have had a similar effect on many around you. Very encouraging."

"So," I was hopeful, "will you help us?"

"Of course," it nodded, "but you are in for one hell of a fight."

"I already guessed as much," I sat back, ready to sign the alliance treaty.

"Once all formalities are taken care of," It concluded, "I shall contact my race and request more soldiers."

"All are welcome," I averred.

I BRIEFED THE GENERAL on all that had been discussed. The evolution discourse. The alliance agreement. The truth about our invaders.

"So," the general scratched his head, "These parasitic assholes usually attack dying races."

"In a sense," I nodded, "mostly ancient races that have refused to give up greed, fear, hate, ignorance, and love of self. According to our new ally, these traits are common within young races such as our own, but very uncommon in the older races."

"So," he assumed, "our best defense, our best weapon, is to cease these traits."

"Yes," I nodded again, "the parasites cannot see advanced races who have evolved past those base negatives."

"Interesting," he mused.

"Yes it is," I agreed.

"And the parasites cannot see you because you are more advanced," he looked at me.

"Precisely," I averred, "and I have had a similar effect on some of the others."

"Well," he chuckled, "of course you do. anyone who isn't changed a bit by your attitude after being around you has a definite problem."

"Meaning?" I was now surprised.

"Meaning that anyone who isn't more positive after being around you has a definite problem," He grinned.

"Really?" I queried.

"Really," He affirmed.

"Didn't know I could affect people that way," I shrugged.

"Keep doing so," He winked, "and we'll all soon be nonexistent to these buggers."

WE QUIETLY SIGNED TREATIES with the remnants over a period of thirty-six days. The rumblings of war were still in the distance, but we needed to be ready. We needed to begin building our legions.

Over the three months that followed, we were joined by at least a dozen more races. Many were from nearby systems that wanted to prevent the spread of the parasite. a few were from more distant systems.

Those who arrived were the advance scouts. They had been sent to weigh the situation and to gather all the information they could, then report back to their leaders. They all realized just how dire the situation was.

All sent warnings home to change. Evolve. All warned that it was the only way to prevent the spread.

All called for reinforcements. We would need as many soldiers as we could get. We would need all the help we could get.

Now, we could only wait. Aggression would only reveal our location. And we could not afford to reveal our location. Not at this point in time.

Training Day

The moments before a war are the bleakest. Darkness seems to settle over everything as uncertainty begins to eat away at resolve and courage. This war was no different.

In a way, it was training day. That long stretch where training took up most of our days, where preparedness met uncertainty. Were we going to be ready when the war knocked at our door? Or would we be too weak to win?

Humanity hung in the balance. Earth hung in the balance. Failure was not an option.

We had no real choice. We had to win or we would cease to be. The Earth was the prize.

I knew I would die trying to save the Earth from being overrun by this infection. I had already decided that. I would not surrender.

I had no clue how the others felt. Only the general seemed to be determined to win or die. The rest, well, most had never fought a war.

Most had never had to face much of anything but a pandemic. Correction. Two pandemics.

The first had been a pandemic of hate that had begun the moment the president had been elected. This one was due to a lack of education. A rash of willful, religiously driven, ignorance.

It swept through the religious community like a wildfire, causing the institutions to fall from favor with the vast majority of the people. Arrogance and greed had made them all bloated, yet empty. Devoid of a soul.

This had made them the perfect target of the alien parasites now invading. Their arrogance. Their hate. Their greed. Their lust for power.

It all made them willing to accept a new master, one that offered to make them all powerful. All knowing. And all seeing. None of which, they would really receive, but they had believed it.

The second pandemic had been a viral one. Those who had bowed to the alien parasites had refused to use common sense and common courtesy. They had seen mask mandates as an infringement on their 'freedoms'. But then, weak minds spawn weak wills. And weak wills generally lead races to their doom.

And humanity was now being led to its doom. Or part of it was. If it survived, it would not remain the same. No, it would forever be altered.

But would we survive? If so, how many of us would remain? One hundred? One million?

"WE'RE NOT SENDING YOU out as a spy anymore," the general stated, looking at me, "your last trips have gained us all the information we need. Our team is busy deciphering much of the video and audio that floods in on a daily basis. We know roughly what the parasite looks like, how it reacts to different physiologies, and roughly how it controls its victim."

"So what is my position now?" I inquired.

"You will be training others how to disappear and become nonexistent to these parasites," he responded, "with the help of our alien allies, of course."

"In other words," I smirked, "you're telling me to train ninjas. Assassins. Shadows."

"Never thought of it like that," he scratched his head, "but yes. That is *exactly* what I am instructing you to do."

"My only question is how many of our current recruits will be willing to drop all animosity and become invisible?" I queried.

"Hopefully, all," He acquiesced, "otherwise, we're FUBAR."

"Not exactly," I smiled, "even one man with a stick can win the day."

"Using my own sayings against me, are you?" He snickered.

"Nah," I chuckled, "just an old line out of a movie."

"Still," he turned away, "I hope that all *do* learn from you and change. It will push the odds of winning more in our favor."

"It will also make men like you and me obsolete once we win," I warned.

"True," he nodded, "but I would rather be obsolete than dead."

"Same here," I averred, "I would rather see mankind rise above all that has kept him divided than to die because he resisted change."

"Change is inevitable," he shrugged, "I believe you told me that. And that which does not embrace change tends to go extinct. This is our extinction scenario."

"And here we were so worried about global warming," I joked.

"We'll have to discuss that when we emerge from this," he admitted.

"That is," I mused, "if we do not learn from our alien allies and adapt their technologies to our needs."

"We would be wise," He began, "if we did learn and adapt."

"When has man ever been willing to learn over his billion or so years of existence?" I tested. "We rise to a certain point, then regress back to the savage we began as."

"DO WE KNOW THEIR PLANET of origin?" I asked one of the aliens sitting in the meeting.

"They originated on a desolate planet in the Sentaire quadrant," the purple colored alien announced, "we were sending out our science teams to explore and map nearby quadrants. Some had landed on a desolate planet and had returned infected."

"So," I began thoughtfully, "your race was the original host?"

"Not the original, no," it responded, "but the original hosts to spread it from planet to planet. We were the first to study it and try to put an end to it. We almost succeeded when it jumped from our race to another nearby race."

"And where, exactly, is this Sentaire quadrant?" I asked.

The alien pulled up a holographic digimap and pointed to a remote region of space on the edge of the known universe that had a very old star at its center.

"That is the Sentaire quadrant," it replied, "why do you ask?"

"So I know where, in relation to my own system, their origin is," I remarked, "and also so we might combat them at their source through sterilizing the planet to destroy all remaining parasites there. I have a hunch that they use a sort of collective consciousness to both communicate and thrive. Perhaps there is a queen of sorts that keeps them all alive."

"You mean," another alien began apprehensively, "like make the planet barren of all life?"

"No," I shook my head, "simply to put an end to the parasite. I realize that life, or nature, is a balancing act. Everything exists for a reason. Even these parasites. But there comes a time when even that must end.

"My proposition is to find an inoculation of sorts, something that kills the parasite only, then release it in massive doses over their planet of origin," I explained, "thus ending the threat. No race deserves to be erased from the universe in this manner."

The Moment Of Truth

War came on swift wings. Like a swarm of hellish locusts, the armies controlled by the parasites swept across the no man's land that separated us from them. War was upon us.

Though empty, we had been scavenging those deserted cities between us and them for food. Those closest to their territory had been picked clean as had those between the Mississippi and the eastern hills. Those closest to us still held enough provisions to keep us fed for a good ten years while those east of the Missouri were almost depleted.

The loss of land to the east left us with everything west of our mountain haven. But there wasn't much to the west. Just deserted farms and ranches that held cattle and rotting vegetables.

We reclaimed these abandoned sources of resources and place garrisons of resistance fighters near them to defend them. these, we would guard from both mountain ranges. To the west, along the western coast, in the mountains, we stationed garrisons of alien allies. Here, they would coordinate the western defenses of our territory.

I admit that we were trusting our allies more than we possibly should have, but we had no choice. There just wasn't enough of us humans to put up a mostly human defense on both borders of our territory. We were forced to give more trust than normal.

But they had not given us any reason to not trust them. They had trained us to use *their* weapons. They had inoculated us with *their* vaccines in hopes of preventing us from becoming infected. most of all, they were helping us develop the weapon we would use to wipe them out completely.

After all, they were fighting to free their planets as well as ours. This was not just Earth's fight. It was for the good of the universe.

If we succeeded, a parasite would be wiped out. If we failed, well, *we* would be wiped out. And if we were wiped out, the parasite might evolve to the point where it could perceive advanced and evolved races and become a menace to all, not just those unwilling to evolve.

And most parasites tended to evolve at some point, just as most viruses did. It was how they remained able to resist any vaccines or medicines created to prevent them. It was nature's way.

But had this parasite been intended to be sentient? Had it been intended to become so complex that it could mimic another race's expectations? Had it been intended to mutate to the point where it intentionally infected races it was never intended to encounter?

I doubted it. I had a feeling that what had been a natural occurrence had become an unnatural threat. This negated all attachment to the natural balance of things.

Thus, it was a threat that needed to be removed from the universe. Something that did not deserve to exist. Like hate, fear, ignorance, and greed. Among other things.

"WE SHOULD EXPECT ATTACKS from both the east and the west," the general began, briefing us on the current position of the alien parasite armies, "we will have to remember that any 'human' soldiers we meet are no longer human. They are infected with the parasite and no longer able to control their own bodies. Just as those who will meet soldiers of their own races will have to remember that they are no longer their comrades.

"It will be difficult to fire upon people you once knew. That is to be expected. But you must view every one that you kill as a mercy killing. You are ending their misery.

"Do not allow them to touch you. I have been told that allowing them to touch will put you at risk of becoming infected. And though you will be wearing body armor, it may not prevent such from happening.

"Remember that you are trying to prevent them from reaching our command center. We cannot afford to allow them to discover what we are developing or planning. Godspeed and God bless."

"Sir," an alien ally began, "should we carpet bomb their front lines as an initial contact? Or as a last resort?"

"Carpet bomb to enforce a distance between," he responded, "in other words do so as an initial attack. Distance between our ground troops and theirs is a must. We cannot allow them to get close enough to spread their infections."

"So," One of our own began, "if they can infect just by touch, why did none of us become infected from the soldiers we captured early on?"

"They were not able to infect," one of our scientists interjected, "The parasite has been evolving and adapting to human hosts. While their first victims had to be intravenously infected while being subjected to electroshock, the first hosts allowed them to begin the adaptation process. This process has made them a contagion that can be passed through touch."

"Well," the man breathed, "fuck me runnin'."

"Can they contaminate the soil?" Another human soldier queried.

"That is not yet known," the scientist admitted, "so we will have to treat it as if they will."

"That is why our team of scientists are trying to come up with a poison or a cure for this," the general answered, "that will wipe out the parasite altogether."

"Why don't we just nuke the bastards?" Another human soldier insisted.

"Because they aren't affected by radiation the way humans are," an alien scientist answered, "we tried radiation therapies in our first attempts to eradicate their threat on our planets. none of those therapies worked. Instead, the parasite adapted."

"So," the first soldier sighed, "it is basically unkillable."

"not at all," I stood, "I killed it with anthrax, malaria, and several other earthbound viruses and parasites. It *can* die from indigenous diseases which it has no immunity to. But it may be able to adapt to and gain immunities eventually. Especially if we overuse the viruses and bacteria. Besides. We also run the risk of succumbing to those viruses and infectious bacteria as well, so it is not safe to use them in mass quantities."

Calm Before The Storm

There is a lull before every battle. A calm that almost makes you believe that there won't be one. It is almost unnerving.

It can fool you into making mistakes. Or into becoming impatient. It can be a source of false hope.

We had entered that short period of time. And yet, none of us seemed to be fooled by it. None of us let down our guard.

We knew our enemy was building up their forces to the east. We knew they had forces to the west. But would they use them all? Where would they strike first?

I had my bets on a united attack, one that hit both sides simultaneously. But were they really that coordinated? Could they pull that off?

I was unwilling to discount any possible move. Their intelligence relied solely on the intelligence of their hosts. Though sentient, they could not be expected to do anything more intelligent than what their hosts could comprehend.

Thus, with those now infected from Earth, The European slaves would be intelligent enough to coordinate an attack while those that had taken our own president and politicians would possibly not be so inclined. After all, they had been less than unified before their infection. Why would they change?

Still, I knew that Yah and Yam were more intelligent and would possibly be in the lead. Had there been a Yah and Yam in charge of the Euro set? What of the Asian set? Or the African set?

Which aliens would be commanding? Which would hide behind the soldiers and allow their puppets to be slaughtered? Would they even care?

And just how sentient were these parasites? The questions seemed to have no end. And no answers. Yet.

My only hope was that the scientists would find some secret weapon we could shoot into the ships and wipe out these abominations. But they would have to make more than one. But how many?

I figured that there was one ship per capital. Maybe one per large city. Byond that, I had no clue.

Did the scientists know? If so, were they developing something they could easily duplicate? Or were they just as in the dark as I was?

"WHAT'S BOTHERING YOU, son?" The general saw that I was puzzled.

"How many ships landed?" I returned.

"From initial accounts," he began, "one per capital. Perhaps the parasite believed, and not exactly or fully wrongly, that all would flock to the capitals when called upon to do so."

"So," I grimaced, "approximately 195 ships. That means 195 dirty bombs."

"Yes," he nodded, "and all sent out as a simultaneous attack."

"A clean sweep," I mused, "providing we don't have any spies in our midst."

"There's always a risk of that," he admitted, "even in the most coordinated and tight knit armies."

"So What's the plan?" I asked.

"We release commands every hour on the hour until the first wave," he stated, "then, when they attack, we begin sending orders as needed. No daily routine. Just every hour."

"And once the enemy is engaged," I filled in the blanks, "we allow the field commanders to do what they have been trained to do."

"Pretty much," he averred, "but under advisement."

"With the main orders being simply to defend and hold their ground," I nodded.

"For as long as they can," he acquiesced, "then they are to retreat only far enough to regroup. There is a 'do not surrender' order included."

"I doubt they will ever surrender, sir," I shook my head, "most are determined to either defeat this enemy or die trying. There is no surrender in them."

"Good," He praised, "let's hope it stays that way until the very end."

"I believe most have the impression that this will not be a brief battle," I opined, "but an extremely long war. Maybe centuries rather than decades."

"And they still stand shoulder to shoulder?" He was incredulous.

"Yes, sir," I nodded in affirmation, "they do."

"Well," he breathed, shocked, "I'll be damned."

"It surprised me too, at first," I stated, "but like them, I am not willing to allow some parasite destroy my planet. Not after what some of us have been trying to do to fix the damage we have already caused."

"I really can't blame you," He allowed, "besides. You've faced worse foes than these in the form of some of your own fellow humans."

"Very true, sir," I smiled, "but hopefully, after this, that will be a thing of the past."

OUR OBJECTIVE WAS TO keep our enemy blind to our plans. There were no written plans. No maps. No clue to what we were up to.

Only those at the core of our command knew anything of what we were planning beyond the day at hand. We sent out hourly rounds of commands to our frontlines. Nothing past the hour.

And since the enemy had yet to attack, the front was only concerned with setting up and readying for the imminent attack yet to come. They had been ordered to stand at the ready, but not to attack. Should the attack start, they were to defend,

At noon, the first wave hit. Our casualties were light. Theirs were not.

I had been correct in assuming that the alien parasite army would try a multi prong attack. They hit us from all sides. North. South. East. West.

Their tactics were weak. Their attack, uncoordinated. Without cohesive leadership.

They were using the human slaves as the coordinators of the battles. Bad choice, but apparently the only one they felt would win the war for them. Distrust among their puppets, though, caused dischord and the inability to make a single cohesive strike.

It seemed that the old rivalries, the old political differences, caused the most problem. None of the human hosts could agree on the most direct way of attacking our front lines. Nor could they agree on which weapons to use.

The resulting chaos was both entertaining and a warning. We had to remain cohesive. We had to continue in our trust of each other. No matter what.

Like A Wave Crashing

We had been expecting their attacks for some time. And yet, they had refrained. We had amassed our army in the time we had. Or, at least, a portion of it.

We would be aided by more extraterrestrial races, but only once the battle had been met. Not until we needed reinforcements. Not until we had turned the tide.

At this point, we remained untested. Untried. We had not tasted battle and were unsure of our resilience.

"I hate silence," the general stated dryly, "the pain of not knowing is worse than discovery."

"I agree, sir," I answered, "the calm before the storm is always worse. But once that wave breaks, we'll know their full strength—and all their weaknesses."

"We have already learned much from them," he affirmed, "plenty that they did not want known. Some that we had our suspicions about."

"I still can't get that poor screaming wretch out of my head," I remarked without warning, "the one from my first vision of how the techno-zombies were made. And that poor scientist who pleaded, through a glance, for me to end his torture of having to attempt the creation of one. Apparently, he was unsuccessful and the aliens took over the process."

"I can't get over the first video of that process I saw," he admitted, "truly sickening. And the video of how they wired up their non-tech non-mindless slaves. **God**, that was horrible!"

"I wouldn't wish that upon my worst enemy," I agreed, "poor saps."

"Poor saps, indeed," he nodded, then changed the subject, "I hope our soldiers have taken to your training. When that first wave hits, they will have to seem invisible enough to take out the enemy without being seen."

"True," I averred, "I hope so as well, sir."

"We'll know soon enough," he sighed.

"And we will know soon enough if we have spies in our midst as well," I reminded him, "the minute we send an order and the enemy anticipates it, we'll know."

"True," he nodded, "God knows they can't get such information from the empty heads of our ex-leaders. The president had never served. The vice president was just as in the dark as the president. And that Secretary of State! How the hell did he get his position?"

"He donated to the president's campaign," I snorted, "just like those who got other cabinet positions."

"Ah, yes," he mused, "and after claiming that the opposition was the goddamn swamp."

"*In coming!!!!*" Came the alarm.

"Well, fuck," he grinned, "can't fault them for not trying."

MISSILES STREAKED TOWARD us. They had used our own weapons against us. The act had not surprised me, since I had often stated that any who desired to defeat us would only have to do just that.

Still, it was a valiant effort. And a failure. After all, they had failed to arm the missiles.

All were either shot down or fell harmlessly to the earth. Then, again, it could have been a diversion. Thankfully, it had not been.

There was a couple hours' pause, then they threw their warcraft at us. Their whole fleet. But we were able to shoot them all out of the sky at a safe distance.

Of course, we fought their warcraft with our own. Their hesitation had given us enough time to duplicate their technologies. And even improve upon them.

Finally, out of desperation, they threw their armies at us. Haphazard. Without a cohesive plan of attack.

Surprisingly, they were initially successful and won the first battle. The loss cost us a thousand men, casualties to a small blunder. But even small blunders had huge costs. And ours had cost us lives.

We would not make the same mistakes twice. Our human soldiers would *follow* the orders of their alien generals, even though they did not like it. They didn't have to like it. They just had to do it.

We would break humanity's arrogance even if it was the last thing we did as a race. We would learn humility no matter the cost. Or we would risk our own extinction.

"How did we do?" The general inquired meekly.

"Fifteen thousand wounded," I sighed, dejectedly, "ten thousand killed. All because of arrogant stubbornness. Two of the worst traits in humanity."

"How many of those were infected by the enemy?" He pressed.

"Don't know yet," I answered, "med techs and the scientists haven't tallied them up yet. Don't know whether we will have those numbers until tomorrow."

"Damn," he stated under his breath, "fucking fools. All of them." He paused. "The cause?"

"A seeming lack of willingness to follow alien generals," I responded, "even though these aliens are far more experienced in the extermination of these monsters."

"Just exactly what we didn't need," he sat down and put his head in his hands, "a bunch of stupid nationalistic bigots. We don't have fucking time for this shit."

"Don't worry, general," I smiled, "once I am done with them, they will know what pain is. I will knock that bullshit out of them before the next wave."

"I sure hope so, Jeff," he looked up at me, "I sure hope so."

"YOUR STUPIDITY IS TO blame for fifteen thousand wounded," I began, "and ten thousand deaths! This is unacceptable!

"But, sir," one soldier interrupted, "these alien bastards are hard to understand."

"Hard to understand my ass," I snorted, "you don't *want* to understand them. And there is where you seriously fuck us up. Your inability to get past the fact that they are *human* is going to be the extinction of the human race. *You* will go down in history as being the reason Earth will be uninhabited.

"Is that what you want? Infamy? Death? Extinction?"

"No, sir!" The chorus of voices rose in the air.

"Then," I scowled, "get your heads out of your asses! You caused casualties! You caused the deaths of some of your compatriots! All because you didn't want to take no orders from no alien!

"Tough! You will continue to take orders from the aliens we have made your generals. Not because you like to do so, but because it will *save your lives*!

"If you want to die so fucking bad, go out there and show the enemy where you are! I'm sure they have snipers just waiting for a chance to use fools like you as target practice! Or get yourself captured! I'm sure they are just waiting for a bunch of y'all to give yourselves up so they can make more soldiers on their side!"

"Please, sir—" one began to plead.

"I think a night of repairing the trenches and burying the bodies will teach you babies a lesson in obedience," I started, cutting off the complaint, "it should also teach you ladies a little humility and respect for authority." I noted their apprehension. "Well? I ain't runnin' no daycare, ***git to work!***"

The soldiers scrambled over each other to get started. I watched their struggle to become a cohesive group and shook my head. If they were any indication of things, we were fucked.

"Is this a bit harsh?" An alien general inquired.

"Nah," I shook my head, "they're lucky I didn't have them dig latrines."

"Latrines, sir?" He/it looked over at me.

"Shit pits," I clarified, "holes over which an outhouse, a portapotty, is placed. One either digs the initial hole or ends up digging the shit out of the hole or buries the current hole after the building is moved. The least likable job in the human army—aside from KP, kitchen duty or cleanup crew."

A Well Oiled Machine

There would be no more hesitancy from the men. Burying those whose deaths they had caused had humbled them. Made them think.

From that moment on, the troops fell in line behind their generals. Over the weeks that followed, they became bonded to their generals. And to each other.

They now knew that they were fighting for something far greater than themselves. They were fighting to save all of humanity. Even those who were now enslaved by the invaders.

This wasn't to say that there weren't occasional bouts of rebelliousness, there were. But for the most part, the mutinous behavior had vanished. The need to dominate had ceased, at least within our army.

In the days that followed, they fought valiantly and without complaint. Where there had been weakness, there was strength. Where there had been rebellion, only obedience.

Soon, the generals began to gain more respect from the men. Their unerring patience and genteel way of dealing with matters proved to be their greatest asset. Their leadership, unparalleled.

As our forces began to gell, they were able to pick out the plants—those sent by the enemy to weaken morale. Those sent to weaken all defenses. Or to sabotage our weapons.

These were taken prisoner and herded into internment camps where they would sit until we decided what needed to be done with them. Or how to free them from the enemy's control. But was that possible?

Could we actually free them? Or were they nulls? Would we erase their ability 'to do' if we removed the enemy's control?

There were so many variables. So many unknowns. We weren't sure that anything would work.

How many of them were acting mindless in order to prove their devotion to these false gods? How many believed that they were going to obtain entrance into Heaven? Or Paradise? Or immortality?

How many were simply foolish enough to believe the lies and think that their daring would gain them princeship? After all, the religious had fallen right in line behind the enemy. They had bowed in worship to these monsters.and less than half had even been 'converted' into the techno-slave or involuntary hosts.

There were still millions, if not billions, of religious worshipers left. Most were already mindless due to their prolonged conditionings by their 'men of God'. some were further conditioned by the propaganda that the former President and his media partners had been piping to them.

These would be willing to attempt sabotage. Or infiltration to cause loss of morale. After all, they had been so willing to kidnap, send pipe bombs, place hate cards in mailboxes, or kill peaceful protestors for the former president, they would definitely be willing to try espionage for their new masters.

They had been so willing to be the reason the country collapsed before the enemy appeared. They would be more than willing to do the same for the enemy. Anything to exact what they perceived as their vengeance.

THE SANDHOGS AND MUDJACKERS had successfully confiscated the heavy equipment needed to build our underground city. Deep beneath the ground, stretching from Colorado to eastern Iowa, and even as far west as Idaho, Nevada, Utah and eastern California, lay a massive city that the enemy could not detect. Nor would it be able to survive the temperatures down there at the entry points. Not even the human hosts could survive the heat.

Not in the ventilation shafts. These, though small, were left open so the city could receive fresh oxygen. The hot air was cooled by our condensers once the air reached the circulation center.

The cities, themselves, were kept inhabitable by alien technology that formed a bio-shield that held in the cooled air. This shield filled only ⅔ of the extremely large cavern, the last third being open and inhospitable. This was intentional.

The unshielded portion of the cavern was meant as a trap. Something to catch the enemy's spies and assassins should they attempt the descent. Here, they would die as they slowly roasted.

The underground city was immaculate. Our alien allies introduced us to generators that could take the heat of magma and turn it into energy. Capacitors were placed to help act as a conduit.this conduit spread the energy out to all the buildings in the city.

A field was created to create a false sun from some of the magma. Then, two. These were darkened just enough to make the 'sun' into a 'moon' so that all could sleep.

Water was piped in from the aquifers in the region. This would give those who sought to be the farmers and ranchers who supplied us with food with waters for their farms and ranches. It would give the rest of us a way to bathe and something to drink.

We had created an inner Earth. And though we fought battles on the surface, this was to be our home for the next four years. Not that it would seem that long. *Or* that short.

Rather, to some, it would seem an eternity. To the rest, it would seem but a blink of the eye. To me, it would end up remaining my home.

But in the beginning, it was home to all. As it had been intended. At the same time, it was a safe haven. A place we could go that our enemy could not.

Some learned to farm in this strange new world. Some would breed cows, pigs, and sheep. All on the outlying rim of the settlement.

Food would still be plentiful. We would be able to eat, even after the crops topside dwindled to nothing. And they were beginning to do just that.

We were, from that point on, self sufficient. We had no need to resurface for supplies. We had all we needed within our new underworld community.

"WE'VE PERFECTED THE dirty bombs," one of the scientists announced, "at least as much as we could without actually testing them."

"Several alien craft were loaded with the vaccine," another scientist added, "and are currently on their way to the parasite's home planet."

"Good, good," the general nodded, "and are the dirty bombs ready to send as care packages to the enemy?"

"Yes," the first scientist averred, "as soon as they are attached to a few missiles. Once that is done, we will be able to send them to each of the enemy craft."

"How long will it take to adapt them to the missiles?" The general sat back.

"A few months," the lead scientist confirmed, "possibly longer."

And what you sent to the parasites' home world?" He pressed.

"Similar to cluster bombs," the lead scientist admitted, "designed to explode on impact, sending up a dust cloud filled with the poisonous mix."

"Should we also bomb Earth?" He was concerned. "To ensure that we kill the parasite here as well? Just in case it can survive in the soil."

"Of course," the lead scientist nodded, "but we'll have to close off our air vents when we do. Or design a filter so that the poison doesn't seep down here."

"Will it wash away?" He was doubtful.

"Yes," the scientist averred, "with the first post war rains."

Escalation

"Here they come!" The warning sounded. "They're throwin' everything they got at us this time!"

"How are the science teams doing on those dirty bombs?" I asked.

"They're almost ready to test," the general answered.

"They better work," I warned, "because we only have one shot."

"Preliminary tests in the lab were positive," he looked at me, "the chemical agent killed the parasite inside the captives we gained from the last clash."

"And the hosts?" I queried.

"It killed them as well," he stated dryly, "that was the only drawback."

"Or, maybe," I smiled, "it was more merciful that it killed them as well. Who knows what kind of side effects the poor devils would have had if they had survived."

"Side effects?" He inquired.

"To the alien parasite," I clarified, "they could have been crippled from the death of the parasite. Or, perhaps, it wasn;t the vaccine but the death of the parasite itself that killed them."

"You mean like a toxin released by a dying parasite as a last ditch effort?" He questioned.

"Precisely," I nodded, "which has been known to happen with certain nematodes here on a rare occasion."

"Never thought of that," he mused, "want me to test your hypothesis?"

"Do we still have live subjects to use as a comparison group?" I asked.

"Of course," he nodded, "and samples from those who died in the tests."

"Have the scientists run the tests," I averred, "I'd like to see what they find."

"Now that you mention it," he grinned, "so would I." As if knowing, one of the scientists appeared. He turned to him. "Run an experiment for us. Run tests on blood and tissue samples from both live parasitic prisoners and the ones killed by the vaccine."

"The purpose?" The scientist inquired.

"Look for any spike in toxins in the blood not related to the vaccine's chemical makeup. Like some nerve toxin that, when in small doses, allows the parasite to control their victim yet, in massive doses, kills."

"You mean like toxins released at massive levels due to death spasms," the scientist nodded, "good call."

"Did you need something?" He asked as the scientist turned to leave.

"I was sent to tell you that we believe the vaccine is ready for use as a chemical weapon on the field," the scientist averred, "but that the missiles are not quite ready. Something to do with the remote detonation mechanism."

"Distribute vaccine grenades to the generals," he commanded, as well as any other form you might have. They will be welcomed additions to their arsenals."

"SIR," THE SCIENTIST returned, "you won't believe this!"

"Well?" The general looked at the man. "Out with it, then!"

"Your idea about the toxins," the scientist began, "you were right!"

"Go ahead," he nodded, "what about it?"

"In the living hosts," the scientist began, "there is an almost imperceptible level of a foreign toxin. It acts almost like a tranquilizer. This toxin, in small amounts is hard to detect as it seems as if the victim's physiology, their bodies, absorbs it and breaks it down almost immediately after it is emitted by the parasite and has done what it is meant to do.

"But in the subjects used to test the vaccine, the toxin is in such massive amounts that it is unmistakable. When the vaccine kills the parasite, the parasite involuntarily releases massive amounts of the toxin! In that massive of an amount, it kills instantly."

"Interesting," I stated, "now run a test of the vaccine after giving the host beta blockers and immunosuppressors. Let us know what that does."

"You should've been a scientist," the man responded, smiling.

"I thought about it once," I replied, "but life just seemed to get in the way of all my plans."

"It does that, sometimes, doesn't it?" he asked.

"It sure does," I nodded, "and you're never the same after."

"No, I wouldn't think so," he shook his head.

I watched him leave. The man was proving a hypothesis for me. If the parasite released toxins to control, and if it involuntarily released them when it died, beta blockers might prevent that release.

It was worth a try. Especially now that the war had gone into high gear. Perhaps it would prove to be more important than I believed. perhaps....

"WE NEED TO SET UP A test of the cure on uninfected humans and aliens from our ranks," I suggested, "we need to form an extra layer of protection for the men and women fighting out there. We need to know that the cure won't kill our soldiers while killing the parasite."

"I would suggest starting with less than a cc of vaccine," the general added, "then work slowly from that."

"Understood, sir," the scientist averred.

"We don't need any deaths from among our own," he warned, "we can't afford to lose anyone. Not to some experiment."

"I understand," the scientist nodded.

"Don't mind him," I smiled, "he's been on edge since things escalated. I believe that what he was trying to say is that he doesn't want any accidents."

"Oh," the scientist mused, "I'm not worried about him. His suggestion about the dosage might be dead on. In fact, I believe that we might have to give small doses to build it up in our immune system slowly."

"Then proceed as you see fit," I nodded, "you don't think that our men are getting residual off the bombs, do you?"

"They might be," he shrugged, "wouldn't know that until we did blood tests."

"Please do," I requested.

He nodded, saluted, then walked away. I watched him go. We knew that the cure, the vaccine, killed the parasite. We only hoped that it wouldn't kill everything else. This was why I had suggested the experiments.

Our cannons and guns were now lobbing dirty shells at the enemy as the war escalated. The smaller air-to-air missiles were the first to be released. These were attached to the converted warcraft and our limited aircraft.

The larger missiles were presenting a problem. Humanity's crude technology was hard for our alien allies to work with. The ones that were to be transported to the parasite's homeworld were not so hard to create.

The cluster bombs were the simplest. They worked on the simple principle that the WWII/Vietnam era cluster bombs worked on. A simple casing holding multiple bombs that were released in mid-air. These smaller bombs would, then, spread out. Sanitizers, we called them.

These were designed for the parasite's homeworld. Our extraterrestrial allies would carpet bomb the planet with these in order to cover every nanometer with the cure. At the same time, we would carpet bomb earth and other planets in hopes of eradicating the parasite completely.

Endgames

The final battle was well planned. Executed to specs, we would possibly never know whether the offworld strikes would work. Everything hinged on it working here on Earth.

At least as far as finding out whether or not the other attacks worked. If it didn't work here, we would never know. We would not survive.

It was determined that the cure was safe for human and alien use and so, they began inoculating all of us. Slowly. Just to allow our bodies enough time to assimilate the vaccine and replicate its antibodies.

I keep calling it a vaccine. It was more of an antibiotic. Something the parasite could not tolerate.

Something that killed the parasite. Destroyed its ability to control. Its ability to invade.

Behind enemy lines, our carpet bombers were laying the gas down thick, killing any larvae that might be on the ground. Our warcraft and planes were blowing their warcraft out of the skies. Our dirty bomb grenades were killing hosts on contact. Our bullets, too.

We were entering the final phase of our little war. From here on, it was either success or humanity was as good as extinct. This was our one shot. Our moment of truth.

"We need to send in a monitor of some sort," I suggested, "to observe when the missile hits the alien ships."

"I agree," the general nodded, "and we can set up an observation system to the west to watch those ships as well."

"Wish I could go," I averred, "but I am needed here. In case this doesn't go as planned."

"Who says you can't go?" He smiled. "After all, this is your baby. Your brainchild. You should be able to witness its success."

"Or its failure," I added.

"Have a little faith in yourself," he advised, "it'll succeed."

"I hope you're right," I smirked, "I'd sure hate to piss off an unseen nest of hornets with a bad idea."

"These parasites are basically vulnerable, Jeff," he reminded me, "and rely on the infected host for mobility and sentience. They ain't gonna live through this. Their slaves might, but they won't. Nor will their hosts."

"You're right," I chuckled, "I was just testing you."

""Oh, har, har," He chided.

"We'll win this thing," I grinned, "even if we have to fight to the very last man."

"Very true," he nodded, "never underestimate the resolve of humanity. We will either succeed or die trying."

I WATCHED AS THE ALIEN ships vanished in the blink of an eye. Those headed for the parasite's homeworld. Those headed for infected worlds.

I pondered just how well our plan would work as I was sped to the south to observe the southern ships. And since I knew that the ships were basically defenseless, without guns or any kind of main defense, I knew that they were all pretty much sitting ducks.

All of the missiles were launched simultaneously and streaked in every direction. I, of course, could not see this as I had already been taken south, but I closed my eyes and imagined how it would have looked. It must have been a beautiful sight. Streaks of fire spreading out like fiery fingers, reaching for their targets.

Below my position, the carpet bombing continued. Behind me, the same. The armies of the alien parasites were being eradicated. Destroyed.

I felt for the hosts. Trapped. Unable to control their own movements. Unable to break free.

We had discovered that the neurotoxin the parasite used acted as an impulse inhibitor. It selected what it wanted its host to do and overrode the impulse so that it could guide its victim's movements. They had no choice but to do.

Those who had rebelled had been killed by the parasites. And though it also killed the parasite within, the collective deemed it necessary. It proved to be a very motivating warning to the rest.

Do not resist or you will be killed. That was the parasite's warning. And after a while, the host was so worn down that they could not resist.

Aware that your body was being used to do evil things and not being able to control it. It was a sad existence, really. If you could call it that.

I called it modified zombification. Living death. A true example of undeath.

Both living and dead, the host struggled with their dilemma. Unable to stop it, they stumbled on in hopes that some other being could. Most would die when their body could take no more of the parasite.

I contemplated this as I watched the alien craft to the south of me. My companion tapped my shoulder and pointed. I turned.

There were the missiles. Coming straight at the craft. I smiled.

I watched as the missiles struck each craft. There was a puff as the missiles slipped into the bubble. Then a loud thud as they pierced the saucer. And finally, a boom of sorts from within the ship.

I watched in disbelief as the ships disintegrated before my eyes. I looked behind me at the lines of alien soldiers. They disintegrated as well.

I VENTURED FORTH FROM my place of concealment with an air tester in hand, my guards by my side. There was no sign of any contaminants. No sign of the parasites.

A single blow seemed to have destroyed them once and for all. Still, I was leery. It seemed too easy. Too good to be true.

I was having a hard time believing that it was over. Nothing had ever been that simple before. Nothing had ended that abruptly.

"Jeff," the general's voice came over my communicator, "did you see that?"

"Yes, sir," I managed, "and I am having a hard time believing my eyes."

"I don't blame ya," he agreed, "never saw anything react that way in my life. They just—melted."

"Yeah," I averred, "I saw that too. Don't know what to make of it."

"Got your sensors going?" He asked.

"Yeah, why?" I returned.

"What are your readings?" He queried.

"Normal," I responded, "no infectious materials, no toxins, no nothin'."

"They're gettin' the same readings from the area to the east," he stated, "almost as if the damn things never existed."

"What of any reports from our alien friends?" I asked, interested.

"Same results," he responded, "apparently, once the carpet bombing began on the parasites' planet of origin, they began disappearing from the other planets."

"So my hunch was right?" I asked.

"Apparently so," he acquiesced.

I sat down where I was and put my head in my hands. My gamble had paid off. My theory had been correct.

Sadly, over a third of the Earth's population as well as the majority of several other planets' populations had had to die before someone figured it all out. Races had been erased. Planets destroyed. Systems drained.

My mind returned to Earth. What had been Earth's civilizations, its countries, had been destroyed. We were now homeless. Without any form of government.

And yet, so many of us had survived from every country. Perhaps we could out back together what had been destroyed. But why?

That had been why we had ended up being noticed. It had drawn the parasite. Our greed. Our hate. Our fear of the unknown. That had been the death of humanity. That had been why the human race had almost been eradicated.

No, we needed a new government. A new path. Something that would lead us forward. Away from those things that we now knew would cause our extinction.